Duma S

Let's live!

Adventures during a time of COVID-19

WRITTEN AND ILLUSTRATED BY NATHI NGUBANE

Featuring Doctor Sam!

Collector's Edition

Duma Says: Let's Live! Collector's Edition

First Published in South Africa by Social Bandit Media in 2021

Edited by Azad Essa

Copy editing & typesetting: Samina Anwary

ISBN: 978-0-620-91593-9

SOCIAL
BANDIT

For children, everywhere.

CONTENTS

Nathi Says:
Why I created this series

HI THERE CHILDREN! MY NAME IS NATHI NGUBANE AND I AM THE AUTHOR OF THE DUMA SAYS BOOK SERIES. I WROTE THESE BOOKS TO REMIND EVERY CHILD AND PARENT TO PROTECT THEMSELVES FROM *THE NASTY CORONAVIRUS.*

DUMA LIVES IN CRAMPED HOUSING, WHERE IT IS ESPECIALLY DIFFICULT TO KEEP SAFE FROM THE VIRUS. HE AND HIS OLDER SISTER ZINHLE AND LITTLE BROTHER WANDILE REALLY CARE ABOUT THEIR COMMUNITY AND THEY WANT TO PROTECT THEIR NEIGHBOURS FROM GETTING INFECTED WITH *CORONAVIRUS.*

10

WHEN I HAVE A COUGH OR HAVE TO SNEEZE, I ALWAYS COVER MY NOSE AND MOUTH SO I CAN *PROTECT THOSE AROUND ME.*

WHENEVER I GO OUT TO THE SHOPS, I ALWAYS WEAR A MASK, KEEP MY DISTANCE FROM OTHERS AND SANITISE MY HANDS.

THE END

My name is Duma and I am ten years old.
I live with my sister Zinhle who is thirteen years old, my brother Wandile, who is six years old, Mama, Baba and our dog Bhubesi.

Since the corona virus came, our lives have changed.
It is such a small virus but it can make us very sick if we are not careful.

I have been sad because I cannot play with my friends.
Wandile is sad that he cannot hug his friends.
Zinhle is also sad that she can't share her lip gloss with her friends.

Mama is a cleaner at the hospital in town. Baba sells fruits and vegetables in town. Every morning they leave for work and Zinhle looks after us.

Our neighbour, Gogo, is very old and has a heart problem. No one is allowed near her these days because the corona virus is dangerous for older people. We don't want to make her sick.

After work, Mama goes to check on Gogo and brings her fresh fruits. Mama leaves the fruits at the door because she can't go into the house.

Every morning, Zinhle goes to collect water from the nearby taps. Some people are wearing masks, some are not. Zinhle made herself a mask using her doek.

Every night, when we have supper, Mama reminds us what she heard at the hospital. "Wash your hands with soap for 20 seconds and cover your mouth when you cough".

Mama also sprays sanitiser she got from work on our hands after we wash them.

One day, while we were in the house, Zinhle had an idea.
"I am going to make masks for the community who don't have masks!" she said.
"That's a good idea! Let's tell Mama and Baba when they get home!" I said.

Later, when Mama and Baba came home, we told them about Zinhle's idea.

"That's a good idea my child!" Baba said.

Mama agreed. "I will ask our church members to give us cloth to help you make the masks, and we can ask Gogo to help too."

The next day, the church ladies dropped off colourful cloth
and elastic bands at our house.
Zinhle left some cloth in a bag outside Gogo's door with a note
asking Gogo to help.

Zinhle started stitching masks and Wandile and I watched her. Zinhle is very good at stitching. She stitched many masks. Wandile and I counted the masks, "1 ....2 ....3 ....4...", but there were too many to count!

Zinhle and Gogo made many masks for the community!
Mama and Baba were so proud.

The next day, Baba and Mama were not working. They decided to give out Zinhle and Gogo's beautiful masks to those that did not have a mask. Zinhle carried Mama's hand sanitiser and sprayed the community members.

Now when Zinhle goes to get water, everyone is wearing masks.
Everyone looks and feels safer, now.

Later that night, Mama reminded us: "Children, what do we do after we have touched everything and before we eat?"

"Wash your hands for 20 seconds with soap, and use hand sanitiser after!" Wandile shouted.

"Yes, my babies. Keep clean and keep healthy. And always wash your hands," Mama said.

35

My name is Duma and I am ten years old.

I live with my sister Zinhle who is thirteen years old, my brother Wandile who is six years old, Mama, Baba and our dog Bhubesi.

Since the coronavirus came, our lives have changed.
It is such a small virus but it can make us very sick if we are not
careful.

Our schools have been closed because of the coronavirus and Wandile, Zinhle and I have been missing school, our friends and our teachers.

Every day Wandile and I play with Bhubesi in our yard.
Zinhle stays indoors and reads her school books.
She loves Mathematics and Technology.

Wandile and I play the same games everyday until we get very bored.

Suddenly I had an idea: If we can't go to school, why can't the school come to us?!

Wandile follows me into the house as I run to talk to Zinhle.
"Zinhle! I have an idea! Let's create classes for the community children!"
"How do we do that?" Zinhle asked.
"You can be our teacher!" I said.

Zinhle smiled. "That is a good idea, little brother! I can teach you Mathematics.

And my friend Lebo can help you with your reading.

Let's tell Mama and Baba when they get home!"

Later, when Mama and Baba came home, we discussed the idea.

"That's a wonderful idea! My children are very smart!" Mama said.

"Well done, Duma! Zinhle, where are you going to have your classes?" Baba asked.

"I don't know yet, but tomorrow, Duma, Wandile and I will go look for a nice place," Zinhle said.

"Ok my children. Don't go too far and don't forget to wear your masks and carry some sanitiser," Mama said.

The next day, we went to look for a place where we can sit and do our classes. We found a spot very close to our home but it was covered in long grass.

"Oh no!" Wandile shouted. "I'm scared of snakes in the bush."

And we laughed.

When we were having supper, Zinhle told Baba about the big grassy area we had found.

"Don't worry my children, I will ask the older boys in our community to cut all the grass," Baba said.

We were so happy. "Thank you baba!" Wandile and I said.

The next day, three strong boys came with their slashers and cut all of the grass. Baba also came, carrying zinc roofing sheets and wooden poles on a wheelbarrow.

"What are those for Baba?" Zinhle asked.

"We are building a shelter to protect you from the rain and hot sun, my dear."

Wandile, Zinhle and I cheered.

Baba and the community elders built our learning shelter.

Baba called us when they were done.

"Wow, baba! It looks so beautiful!" Zinhle said.

"I can't wait to start teaching the community children with Lebo!"

Baba placed a large mat on the floor and then marked it with chalk.

Each of us had to wear a mask and sit separately from each other.

Zinhle made a register for the classes. Classes for us will happen in the mornings. And in the afternoon, the older children will have their classes.

Our first class was so much fun. Zinhle taught us how to add and subtract.

And Lebo read us a story. And asked us many questions.

It was time for the older children and their lessons. They did big-school Mathematics and it looked difficult! But they enjoyed it because Zinhle and Lebo were very good play teachers!

The classes went on for many days until school reopened.

And if schools close again, we know what to do.

"Zinhle, the community is very proud of you and your classes. Everybody is saying that their children are much happier and they get to see each other!" Mama said.

"Well done my children I am so proud of all of you!" Baba said.

"You bring us joy. You bring us hope. And most of all, you make us look forward to tomorrow!"

HEY KIDS, IT'S ME DOCTOR SAM AGAIN. I KNOW SCHOOL FEELS VERY DIFFERENT THESE DAYS.

BUT REMEMBER, THE MOST IMPORTANT THING IS TO KEEP YOUR EDUCATION GOING. KNOWLEDGE IS POWER! IF YOU ARE HOME, DON'T FORGET TO KEEP STUDYING. IF YOU ARE AT SCHOOL, DON'T FORGET TO WASH YOUR HANDS AND KEEP *YOUR SOCIAL DISTANCE.*

My name is Duma and I am ten years old.
I live with my sister Zinhle who is thirteen years old, my brother Wandile who is six years old, Mama, Baba and our dog Bhubesi.

Since the coronavirus came, our lives have changed. It is such a small virus but it can make us very sick if we are not careful.

Every day, Wandile and I have breakfast and get ready to go to the learning shelter.

We sing our favourite songs and Lebo reads us our favourite stories.

Not a day passes without learning something new. And not a day passes without Wandile reminding us he can count to one hundred. Eish!

One day while we were in the learning shelter, Zinhle made an announcement:

"Bantwana, today we are going to do something different."

'Yes, today we will be ... playing GAMES!" Lebo said.

"Games? What kind of games?" Wandile asked excitedly.
Zinhle laughed. "Have some patience, Bhuti!"
All the children laughed, too.

"Quieten down, everyone!" Lebo said.

"We need to remember a few things before we get started."

"That's right," Zinhle said. "What games can we play during this time of the coronavirus?" Zinhle asked.

"Tag!", my friend Jabulani shouted.

"Ey, Jabulani, what are you saying?" I said.

"If we play tag we have to touch each other. We can't play that."

"So your homework, bantwana, is to come up with a game we can play during this virus" Zinhle said. "Remember no contact games." Yes, we must all protect one another from the spread of coronavirus!" Lebo added.

Later that night, while we were having supper, I approached my sister. "Zinhle, I think I have a game we can play and also keep our social distance!" I said.

"Good, little brother! You must tell us tomorrow in class" Zinhle smiled. Mama and Baba also smiled to each other.

The next day, Zinhle, Wandile, the community children and I gathered outside the learning shelter. "Ok bantwana, which games can we play to keep us socially distanced?" Lebo asked.

"Hide and go seek!" Shouted Jabu.

"Good one Jabulani! We can play "hide and go seek" without touching one another!" Zinhle clapped.

"Which other game can we play without touching each other?" Zinhle asked.

"Rope skipping!" Thombi, one of the children shouted.

"Yes! Two of you can wave the rope and one can jump, keeping social distance! Very good!" Zinhle said.

"We need one more game. Who has another idea?" Zinhle asked.

"Soccer!" I said. Zinhle looked at me.

"But Duma, when you boys play soccer, you're always falling on top of each other".

Everyone laughed. I tried to explain: "I mean we can practise our passing and shooting."

Zinhle smiled. "Okay little brother, training for the next soccer season it is! Maybe the girls can train you!" Everyone cheered.

Zinhle and Lebo divided us into three groups.
"Remember to social distance and come sanitise your hands after the games!" Zinhle said.

Group One played hide and go seek.
Wandile was a natural when it came to hiding in the bushes.

Group Two took turns rope skipping. Group Three practiced their passing and shooting. I was in group three! I love soccer!

After our games, Zinhle and Lebo called us to wash our hands
and apply hand sanitiser.
"That was a lot of fun Zinhle!" Wandile cheered.
"Yes, it was! Tomorrow, we start again."

6 STEPS TO CLEAN HANDS

1 Wet your hands

2 Use soap

3 Scrub for 20 seconds

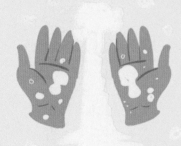

4 Rinse your hands

5 Dry hands with clean towel

6 Your hands are clean!

Acknowledgements

There were many hands involved in this project and without their efforts we would not have completed this adventure.

I would like to thank Karabo Kgoleng and Thabiso Mahlape for their feedback and guidance when we first came up with the idea of creating free resources for children during this extraordinary time of the coronavirus. Then there was Dr Sameera Essa and Dr Shenaaz Essa and Dr Shehnaaz Peer for their medical advice. Following the publication of the first book, our work received an immense boost from South Africa's Department of Health who opted to endorse the book and put it on their zero-rated website. This meant that the book was accessible to millions without requiring data. Thank you for Hasina Kathrada and Naeem Mayat for making this possible. I would also like to thank librarians at the New York City School library system as well as the Centre for African Studies at Harvard University for featuring 'Duma Says' in their list of free covid-19 resources.

In order for the books to travel far and wide, this wouldn't have been possible without the translations from Nokubonga Gasa (isiZulu), Bongisisa Mamba (isiXhosa), Nasra Bwana (Kiswahili) and Pioneer Printers (Braille). You made it possible for the books to be read in languages spoken in the homes of millions of children.

A special thanks to everyone who contributed to the GoFundMe project that has helped us expand this project into three stories. These include: Aadila Sabat, Saadia Toor, Haseena Jamal, Tariq Syed , Shehnaaz Peer, Aadil Rashid Mir, Kathrin Lehel, Nouran El-Hilali, Ben Williams, Sarwat Malik-Hassan, Rehana Qadir, Karim Shah, Sana Uddin, Mohamed Nanabhay, Marina Sofi, Sadaf Haider, Mohammed Kanjwal, Syed Hassan, Shalini Kishan, Jacob Lief, Laila Arian & Imad Musa, and a number of other anonymous donors

And finally, this project could not have been done without the support of Samina Anwary for the typesetting, layout and coolness of the final product and Jane Harley for offering her services to prepare the books as e-books and print-ready.

Finally, I would like to thank my friend Azad Essa, my parents Bongiwe Ngubane and Vusumuzi Makhathini for their continued support and encouragement in the pursuit of this important project.

SOCIAL BANDIT

Made in the USA
Monee, IL
01 March 2021